It takes a year to fly to Mars, ... ky things. Too much pressure and
I'm glad we didn't go to Jup... ~~~~~ {BL

I'm BORED!!!

Dad said there is a face on
Mars but I haven't seen it.

This is DAVEY MARTIN'S
MARS JOURNAL
(TOP SECRET!)

There's not very much
gravity on Mars. Things
are easy to lift. I don't weigh
hardly anything!

Everything here is RED!!

Sometimes it is too cold to go outside so we stay
inside and play checkers and
I always pick BLACK!

Mars has
2 moons →

Phobos Deimos

Mom thought the trailer was fine
the way it was but Dad got his way. →

There are
NO hamburgers here!

I don't know why I brought
my swimming trunks. →

It's a good thing
planets are round
because they are
easier to draw →

mercury
venus earth mars
asteroids
jupiter
Saturn
uranus neptune
pluto is a dwarf
?

Little, Brown and Company

Hachette Book Group USA
237 Park Avenue, New York, NY 10017
Visit our Web site at www.lb-kids.com

First Edition: February 2008

Library of Congress Cataloging-in-Publication Data

Gall, Chris.
  There's nothing to do on Mars / written and illustrated by Chris Gall—1st ed.
    p. cm.
  Summary: After moving to Mars with his family, Davey complains of being bored until he
begins exploring the planet with his dog Polaris and uncovers a most unusual "treasure."

  ISBN-13: 978-0-316-16684-3
  ISBN-10: 0-316-16684-7
  [1. Mars (Planet)—Fiction.] I. Title. II. Title: There is nothing to do on Mars.
  PZ7.G1352Thn 2007
  [E]—dc22   2006025290

10 9 8 7 6 5 4 3 2 1

CPI

Printed in China

The illustrations for this book were done by hand engraving clay-coated
board and processing the result with the same space-age device used by
NASA to help send men to the moon.

The text was set in ITC Benguiat Gothic, and the display type is Insignia.

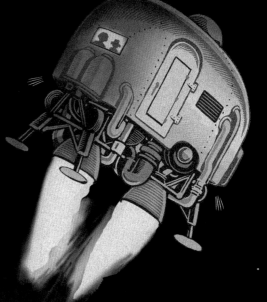

For Kylie, Amanda, and Gavin

THERE'S NOTHING TO DO ON MARS

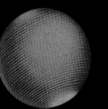

written and illustrated by

CHRIS GALL

LITTLE, BROWN AND COMPANY
New York ⚭ Boston

When Davey Martin's family moved to Mars, he thought he'd never make a friend again.

"You'll be fine!" his father said.

"You've got your dog," his mother said.

"There's lots to do on Mars!" they insisted.

But Davey knew there was nothing to do on Mars.

The nights were very cold.

The dust storms were terrible.

And there was no water anywhere.

"I'm bored!" Davey shouted one day.

"Go out and play!" his father shouted back.

Davey hopped on his scooter. His dog, Polaris, chased after him.

"Okay, you know the rules," Davey reminded Polaris. "Don't bark at the moons and be careful what you sniff—you might overload your circuits."

Polaris couldn't fetch, and sometimes his batteries leaked all over the floor, but he did have a remarkable nose. Once he even smelled some old socks Davey left behind on Earth.

Polaris beeped and clicked, and together they raced across Mars.

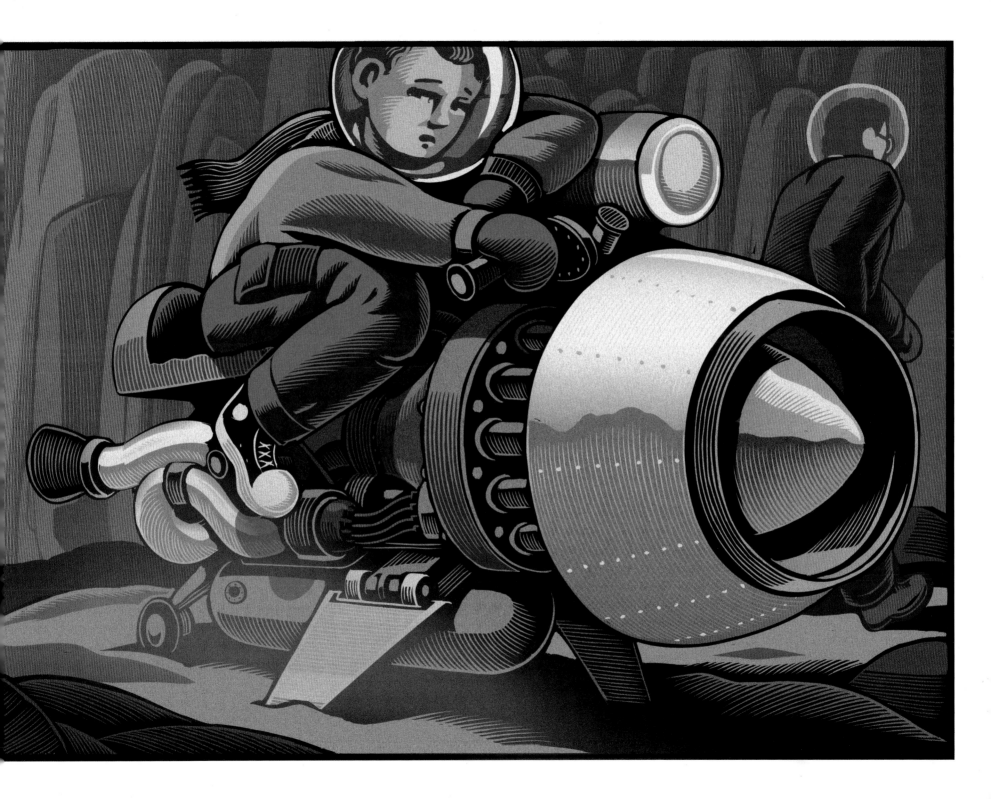

They zoomed over dry riverbeds, zipped through deep canyons, and zigzagged around giant craters. They even spotted some ancient volcanoes.

"I'm bored," Davey said. "Let's climb a tree!"

The tree they found had been thirsty for many years and had become quite cranky. And when the tree began to moan and groan and shake its brittle branches, Davey quickly jumped down.

"I'm bored!" Davey said. "Let's build a fort!"

Thanks to the light Martian gravity, Davey found the rocks easy to lift.

"It's not a bad fort, I guess, but why do all the rocks on Mars have to be red?" Davey grumbled.

From high up on the steps, Polaris noticed a horrible stench coming from the valley. He whirred and clattered with excitement.

"Martians!" Davey shouted.

The Martians had not been able to take a bath in a very long time, and they smelled worse than skunks. Davey and Polaris joined them in a big rain dance anyway, hopping and howling like real Martians.

Soon the stink of Martians became too much. When Polaris began to wobble and stagger, Davey thought it might be time to sneak away.

"I'm bored," Davey whispered. "Let's dig for buried treasure!"

Polaris sniffed out a good
spot and started to dig.

All he found was an
old bone.

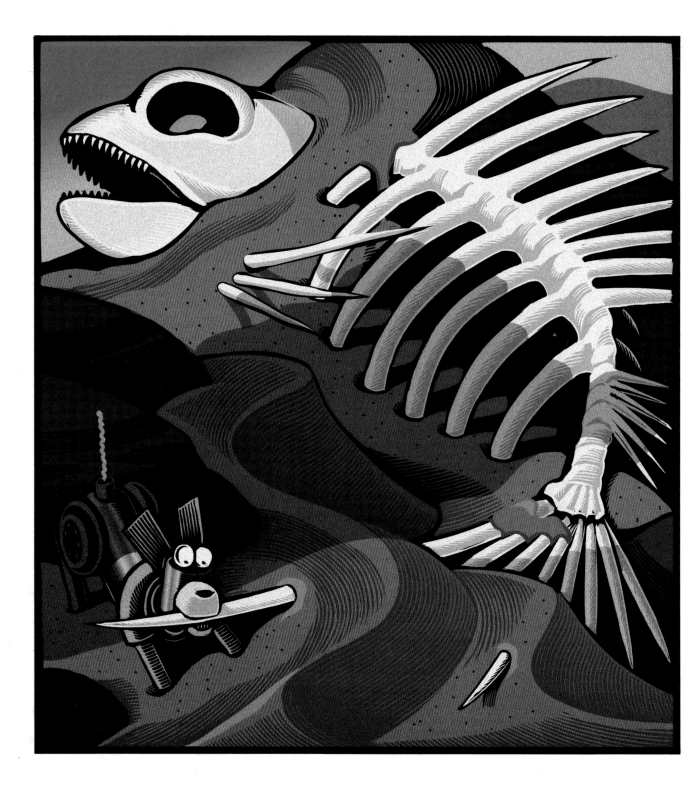

All Davey found was an old toy.

Suddenly, Polaris sat up and put his nose into the thin Martian air. He buzzed and bleeped and bolted for the horizon.

"Find the treasure!" Davey called, and sped after Polaris, who was bounding toward the most extraordinary mountain on Mars.

At the very top of the mountain Polaris and Davey began digging furiously in the center of a great crater.

The more they dug, the softer the dirt became, until the ground began to crack and hiss and shake like pudding.

Polaris's batteries started to leak.

Davey's stomach did a somersault.

They dashed for the scooter and just as Davey reached for the handlebars…

Water rushed down the canyons, raced through the riverbeds, and flooded into empty oceans. The scooter screamed ahead of the crashing waters. Davey didn't dare look back. He could hear the roar right behind him.

Later that day, Davey and Polaris bounded through the door.

"Well, young man, did you find something to do?" his mother asked.

Polaris sneezed. Davey smiled. Red mud oozed out of his pants. His mother turned around slowly and peered out the door.

"Oh, my," she said.

At first, everybody was happy to have water back on Mars—especially because the Martians started bathing again. No one was happier than Davey, who spent much of his time surfing.

But soon many more people came from Earth. And they came with ships and hotels and sunscreen.

"Oh, dear," Davey's mother sighed one day. "I miss our old Mars without so many people around."

"Maybe we should move to Saturn," Davey's father suggested, and Davey's eyes grew big.

Davey knew there was NOTHING to do on Saturn!